E MOO
Mooser, Stephen
Smell that clue!

102407

Put Beginning Readers on the Right Track with
ALL ABOARD READING™

The All Aboard Reading series is especially designed for beginning readers. Written by noted authors and illustrated in full color, these are books that children really *want* to read—books to excite their imagination, expand their interests, make them laugh, and support their feelings. With fiction and nonfiction stories that are high interest and curriculum-related, All Aboard Reading books offer something for every young reader. And with four different reading levels, the All Aboard Reading series lets you choose which books are most appropriate for your children and their growing abilities.

Picture Readers
Picture Readers have super-simple texts, with many nouns appearing as rebus pictures. At the end of each book are 24 flash cards—on one side is a rebus picture; on the other side is the written-out word.

Station Stop 1
Station Stop 1 books are best for children who have just begun to read. Simple words and big type make these early reading experiences more comfortable. Picture clues help children to figure out the words on the page. Lots of repetition throughout the text helps children to predict the next word or phrase—an essential step in developing word recognition.

Station Stop 2
Station Stop 2 books are written specifically for children who are reading with help. Short sentences make it easier for early readers to understand what they are reading. Simple plots and simple dialogue help children with reading comprehension.

Station Stop 3
Station Stop 3 books are perfect for children who are reading alone. With longer text and harder words, these books appeal to children who have mastered basic reading skills. More complex stories captivate children who are ready for more challenging books.

In addition to All Aboard Reading books, look for All Aboard Math Readers™ (fiction stories that teach math concepts children are learning in school); All Aboard Science Readers™ (nonfiction books that explore the most fascinating science topics in age-appropriate language); All Aboard Poetry Readers™ (funny, rhyming poems for readers of all levels); and All Aboard Mystery Readers™ (puzzling tales where children piece together evidence with the characters).

All Aboard for happy reading!

For my two ace kids, Chelsea and Bryn—S.M.
To Mrs. Joyce Fogo, my art teacher at Sam
Rayburn High School, Pasadena, Texas.
Wherever she is—B.B.

GROSSET & DUNLAP
Published by the Penguin Group
Penguin Group (USA) Inc., 375 Hudson Street, New York, New York 10014, U.S.A.
Penguin Group (Canada), 90 Eglinton Avenue East, Suite 700, Toronto, Ontario, Canada M4P 2Y3
(a division of Pearson Penguin Canada Inc.)
Penguin Books Ltd, 80 Strand, London WC2R 0RL, England
Penguin Ireland, 25 St Stephen's Green, Dublin 2, Ireland
(a division of Penguin Books Ltd)
Penguin Group (Australia), 250 Camberwell Road, Camberwell, Victoria 3124, Australia
(a division of Pearson Australia Group Pty Ltd)
Penguin Books India Pvt Ltd, 11 Community Centre, Panchsheel Park, New Delhi - 110 017, India
Penguin Group (NZ), Cnr Airborne and Rosedale Roads, Albany, Auckland 1310, New Zealand
(a division of Pearson New Zealand Ltd)
Penguin Books (South Africa) (Pty) Ltd, 24 Sturdee Avenue, Rosebank, Johannesburg 2196, South Africa

Penguin Books Ltd, Registered Offices:
80 Strand, London WC2R 0RL, England

Text copyright © 2006 by Stephen Mooser. Illustrations copyright © 2006 by Brian Biggs. All
rights reserved. Published by Grosset & Dunlap, a division of Penguin Young Readers Group,
345 Hudson Street, New York, New York 10014. ALL ABOARD MYSTERY READER and
GROSSET & DUNLAP are trademarks of Penguin Group (USA) Inc. Printed in the U.S.A.

Library of Congress Cataloging-in-Publication Data

Mooser, Stephen.
Smell that clue! / by Stephen Mooser ; illustrated by Brian Biggs.
p. cm. — (All aboard mystery reader. Station stop 3) (Goofball Malone ace detective)
Summary: When his class wins a free trip to the circus, Goofball gathers clues to track down
the winning number his teacher must produce.
ISBN 0-448-43912-3
[1. Lost and found possessions—Fiction. 2. Teachers—Fiction. 3. Schools—Fiction. 4. Clowns—
Fiction. 5. Riddles—Fiction. 6. Mystery and detective stories.] I. Biggs, Brian, ill. II. Title. III.
Series.
PZ7.M78817Sm 2005
[Fic]—dc22
                                        2005013145

10 9 8 7 6 5 4 3 2 1

GOOFBALL MALONE
ace detective

SMELL
THAT
CLUE!

By Stephen Mooser
Illustrated by Brian Biggs

Grosset & Dunlap

Chapter 1: A Strange Morning

"Okay, class," our teacher, Ms. Peck, said. "It's time for independent reading. That means we read quietly at our desks. No talking, no laughing, no . . ."

HONK! HONK! HONK! A loud noise, from outside the classroom, interrupted her. What could be making that noise? *HONK! HONK! HONK!* We heard it again. Ms. Peck pushed her glasses up on her forehead, and calmly said, "Come in!"

The door flew open. A blue-nosed clown in polka-dotted pants burst into the room.

"Yikes!" I yelled. What in the world was a *clown* doing in our classroom?

"Howdy!" shouted the clown. He gave his fat nose a squeeze. *HONK!* A second later the polka-dotted clown tumbled onto Ms. Peck's desk and stood on his head. Ms. Peck giggled. She giggled at everything. Everyone else just screamed.

Ms. Peck clapped her hands. "This morning we have a very special visitor from the circus, but before I introduce our guest, I have a funny circus riddle.

Who can tell me why the polka-dotted clown can never hide?"

"Goofball knows! He's king of the riddles!" shouted Teensie Wigglesworth. Teensie sat in my row. There was a bow in her hair the size of a pinwheel. She thought it made her look tall. I thought it made her look silly. But I didn't say so. We were best friends.

"Okay, Goofball, what's the answer?" asked Ms. Peck.

I know every joke and riddle there is.
That's why everyone calls me Goofball.
Also, of course, because of my spiky
hair, plaid pants, and big glasses. I was
thinking as hard as I could. The answer
was hanging on the tip of my tongue.
But I couldn't seem to get it to fall off.

I shook my head and sighed.

No one else knew either.

Just then, the clown somersaulted off the desk. He stood up and squeezed his nose. *HONK!* "Wonder what I'm doing here?" he asked. "Who can solve the mystery of the silly clown?"

"Me! Me!" I yelled. I pulled a silver badge out of my pocket and showed it to the clown. "I'm Goofball Malone, Ace Detective."

But, before I could guess, the clown gave away the answer.

"And I'm Pupu the clown," he said. "I'm here to give you tickets to the circus."

Everyone cheered. Teensie clapped so hard, her giant bow wiggled in her hair. Walter Dobbs kicked his foot in the air. Whoops! His shoe flew off and landed in the aisle.

"Walter, put on your shoe," said Ms. Peck.

"Please," said Teensie. She made a face. "Your sock stinks!"

Walter quickly put his shoe back on.

"You're getting tickets because the circus held a special contest," explained Pupu. "We mailed every teacher in town a piece of paper. This piece of paper had a picture of a clown holding up a ball with a number on it. Then we had a drawing. The teacher with the winning number got circus tickets for his or her whole class. Guess who won?"

"I did!" said Luann. She fluffed her hair and smiled. "I win everything."

"I did," said Walter. "Hooray!"

"Walter didn't win. Neither did Luann. This is an easy mystery to solve," I said. "Remember, only teachers got numbers. Look around. There's only one teacher in the room. That means Ms. Peck is the winner."

"That's right," said Pupu. "You *are* an ace detective."

I stood up and took a bow. Everyone clapped.

The clown squeezed his nose three times.
HONK! HONK! HONK!

Everyone got quiet.

"Last night, the circus called Ms. Peck and told her she had won," said Pupu. "They sent me here to get the piece of paper with the winning number on it." He stuck out his hand. "When Ms. Peck gives me the piece of paper, everyone will get their circus tickets."

"I have it right in here!" said Ms. Peck. She lifted up a big brown purse from under her desk. She unzipped the top. Then she reached inside. "Hmmm," she said, fumbling around. "I know it was here this morning." She looked and looked. Then she looked some more. Still no piece of paper.

I'd never seen Ms. Peck so confused, or so worried.

"This is terrible," she said.

For a second I thought she might cry. Me too. More than anything I wanted to go to the circus. What was Ms. Peck going to do?

Chapter 2: On the Case

Ms. Peck turned over her purse and gave it a shake. Everything tumbled onto her desk. Lipstick. Pencils. Car keys. Coins. Everything but what she was looking for.

Teensie poked me in the back. "Ms. Peck's purse smells like rose perfume. I love it." Teensie was the best smeller in the class. Not even dogs could smell as well.

"I had it this morning. I know it," Ms. Peck said.

"Maybe it was eaten by bugs!" shouted Luann.

"A monkey borrowed it!" shouted Teensie.

"I bet it was stolen!" yelled Walter. "Let's call the police!"

"We don't need to call anybody," I said. "Don't forget we have a real detective right here in the room." I flashed my badge to the class again. "I can solve anything."

Walter laughed. "You can't even solve Ms. Peck's riddle."

I jumped up and faced the class. "Come on. Give me a chance. I know I can find that missing piece of paper."

Teensie stood up and wrapped her arm around my shoulder. "Goofball is our riddle king," she said. "And everybody knows riddles are just tiny mysteries. He's the best detective in class."

"He's the *only* detective," mumbled Walter.

"All right, Goofball, the job is yours," said Ms. Peck. "We're counting on you."

"I must have that slip of paper by one o'clock today, right after lunch," said Pupu. "Otherwise, I'm afraid we'll have to pick another winner."

I gave the class a salute. "I'm on the case. It can't hide from me."

Teensie slapped me on the back. "Goofball won't fail us."

"He'd better not," said Walter.

Walter was right. If I couldn't find the paper, everyone was going to blame me for sure. Me and my big mouth.

Chapter 3: Clues and a Suspect

Just then the bell rang. It was lunchtime. Everyone ran out of the room. Everyone but me and Teensie.

"Lunch can wait," I said. "Right now we've got a case to solve."

Ms. Peck was busy writing in a book. When we went up to her desk she put a bookmark on the page. Then she closed the cover.

"I feel terrible," she said. "Where could I have lost that paper? I don't have a clue."

"That's not true. I bet you have lots of clues," I said. I pulled a red notebook from my back pocket. It said *Goofball Malone, Ace Detective* on the cover. I wrote all my clues inside. I wrote my jokes and riddles in there, too, including the clown riddle Ms. Peck had just told the class.

"Now, please tell me when you last saw that piece of paper. Then tell me where you've been since then."

"Hmmm, let's see," said Ms. Peck. She rubbed her chin and thought. "I put the winning number in my purse this morning. I remember zipping the purse up tight. Then I drove to school."

I was writing as fast as I could.

"I parked the car and went in to see my best friend, Nurse Looper," she continued. "I wanted to tell her the good news."

"Was anyone else in the nurse's office?" I asked.

"Yes, Billy Puker. He had a scraped elbow."

Billy Puker was a big bully in the grade above me. The students didn't call him Billy, though. They called him Puke. I didn't like him one bit. He didn't like me either.

"Was Puke ever alone with the purse?" asked Teensie.

"Just for a minute when Nurse Looper and I went to the back room," said Ms. Peck.

"Uh-huh," I said. I wrote down the word Suspects. Under it I wrote Puke.

"Where did you go next?" I asked.

"I went to the library to look up the clown riddle," she said.

"Then what?" I asked.

"The bell rang, so I hurried to class," said Ms. Peck. She shook her head and fought back a tear. "Is there any way I can help you find it?"

"You've been a big help already," I said, looking over my list of clues.

Before I closed my book, Ms. Peck picked up a piece of paper and tore it in two.

"Bookmarks are very important. I use them all the time." She handed me a piece of paper. "Here, put this on your clues page. That way you can quickly find what you need."

"Thanks," I said. "Every second counts."

Teensie blushed. "I love your perfume. I smelled it when you opened your purse."

Ms. Peck blushed, too. "The perfume spilled inside my purse last night. Now everything in it smells like roses." Ms. Peck giggled. "Your nose tells you everything, doesn't it?"

"Sometimes more than I want to know," said Teensie. "I already can tell that lunch will be awful. I've smelled it all morning. It's macaroni, cheese, pickles, and pineapple—all mixed up."

"No pickles and pineapple for me," said Ms. Peck. "Today I feel like a sandwich."

"Funny, you don't look like a sandwich," I said.

Teensie laughed at my joke.

But Ms. Peck was too upset to even giggle.

Chapter 4: The First Clue

Teensie and I went out of the classroom. Springtime was in the air—and on the walls. Paper flowers were taped up along the hallway. A yellow sun hung from the ceiling. Cardboard tulips were pinned to the doors. But there was no time to enjoy the view. We had a case to solve.

The nurse's office had been Ms. Peck's first stop. Now it was our first stop, too.

We knocked on the door and went in. Nurse Looper was at her desk.

"Are you sick?" asked Ms. Looper. "Shall I take your temperature?"

"Don't you have one of your own?" I asked. "Why do you need to take mine?"

Teensie laughed, but not Ms. Looper. She'd heard the joke before. From me.

"Ms. Peck lost her winning number for the circus lottery," explained Teensie. "Maybe she lost it in here."

"Lost it here? I don't think so. Her purse is always zipped up. And besides, I would have seen it on the floor," she said.

I looked around the office. The floor was spotless—and paperless.

"Ms. Looper, what about Puke?" asked Teensie. "Did he unzip the purse?"

"I don't think so," she said. "Puke is not a thief."

I winked at Teensie. Ms. Looper was a good nurse, but she was not a good detective. Puke was still a suspect. And if he did take the ticket, I already knew how to prove it. I pulled out my book. I turned to my page of clues. It was easy to find, thanks to the bookmark.

1. Put number in purse.

2. Purse was zipped up.

3. ~~Went to nurse's office.~~

4. Puke alone with purse.

5. Went to library to
   find riddle.

6. Bell rang.

7. Hurried back to class.

Something was missing besides the winning number. But I didn't know what it was. Yet.

"Do you need to know anything else?" asked Ms. Looper.

"Yes," I said. "Do you know why the polka-dotted clown can never hide?"

"No, why?" she replied.

"I don't know either," I said. "It's very embarrassing. I'm king of the riddles, but I can't figure it out."

I looked up at the clock. Time was running out. We needed that piece of paper, and soon. Otherwise another class would win the prize. It was time to find my number-one suspect, and I knew just where he was . . .

Chapter 5: Suspect Number One

We hurried down the hall to the cafeteria. When we got to the lunchroom Teensie pinched her nose. "Eeeyew! This place stinks. Pineapple and pickles is a horrible combination."

We looked around. Trays clattered. Food splattered. Everywhere kids chattered. Over to the side the lunch ladies were starting to clean up. Walter Dobbs saw us across the room and waved. I was about to wave back when I saw someone else. It was Billy Puker. He had sneaked up behind Walter and was about to snatch his carton of milk.

"Hey, Puke!" I yelled, catching his attention. Everybody else looked up, too. When you yell the word *puke* in our cafeteria, people get nervous.

"Get away from that milk!" I said, quickly crossing the room.

"Goofball, be careful," said Teensie. She sounded funny because she was still pinching her nose. "Puke is dangerous."

He looked worse than dangerous. When I came up alongside him he pulled back his lips and snarled. With his pushed-in nose and chipped front tooth, he reminded me of a bulldog. He made two fists and waved them in my face.

"What do you want, Goofball?"

"I don't want anything," I said calmly.

We stared at each other for a moment. Then I gave him a big smile, turned, and quickly walked away.

Teensie hurried after me. "Wait. Where are you going? Why didn't we question Puke?"

"We didn't need to," I said. I took out my book and crossed out Puke's name. "Puke never put a hand in Ms. Peck's purse. I'm positive."

"How can you be positive?" said Teensie. "He was alone with it."

"He can't be the thief. And if your finger hadn't been pinching your nose, you would know it, too."

Teensie took her finger off her nose and thought about it.

"The solution was simple," I explained as we headed toward our next stop, the library. "Everything that had been inside Ms. Peck's purse that day smelled like perfume. When Puke waved his fists in my face I didn't smell anything. So, he couldn't have had his hands in that purse or on that paper."

"Excellent work," said Teensie. "So now we know he didn't take it. It's lucky you spotted him when you did."

I took two more steps then skidded to a stop. "That's it!"

"That's what?" said Teensie.

"Spotted! That's the answer to the riddle! The polka-dotted clown can never hide because he will always be spotted!"

Teensie laughed.

Just then the first bell rang. There were only seven minutes until one o'clock. Seven minutes until another class would win the tickets. And, if I couldn't find the lost paper, seven minutes until disaster.

Chapter 6: Mr. Bean's Books

My list of clues was shrinking fast. The library had been Ms. Peck's last stop that morning. Now it was our last hope. When we dashed through the door I saw the librarian, Mr. Bean, sitting on the carpet putting away books in the jokes and riddles section. He looked up when we walked over. "No time to check out a book," he said. "The first bell just rang."

"We don't need a book," I said, looking down at the fuzzy ring of gray hair around his bald head. "We need to know if you saw Ms. Peck earlier today."

Mr. Bean squinted. "What is this about, Goofball?"

"It's about a valuable piece of paper," I said. "Ms. Peck may have lost it here in the library."

"She was certainly near this shelf," said Teensie. "I smell her perfume."

Mr. Bean nodded. "She was here before school started," he said. "But she didn't stay long. When the bell rang she raced off to class. I would have noticed if she dropped anything."

I looked around. If the paper was there, I didn't see it.

"Now get going," said Mr. Bean. "You're going to be late for class."

I felt horrible. Because I couldn't solve
the mystery, our class was not going to the
circus. I took a deep breath then opened
my book for one last time to the clues
page. The page was easy to find, thanks
to Ms. Peck's bookmark. I studied it. Just
about every clue had been crossed out.
Puke had not taken the paper. It had not
fallen out in the nurse's office. It wasn't
on the floor of the library either. I was
just about to give up when suddenly, I
slapped a hand against my cheek and
gasped.

"Oh, my!" There, right in front of me was the most important clue of all. I don't know how I had missed it!

"Amazing!" I muttered. All this time the answer to the mystery had been stuck in my book. In fact, Ms. Peck had given it to me herself.

Teensie put a hand on my shoulder. "It's two minutes to one. I guess we better go tell our class the sad news."

"Maybe not," I said. "Just hold on a minute."

I turned quickly to Mr. Bean. "I need a book, fast. Something with clown riddles in it."

Mr. Bean pulled out a book called *Silly Circus Riddles*. "How about this?" he said.

"This looks about right," I said. I
quickly turned to the chapter called
"One Hundred Clown Riddles." It wasn't
hard to find. Ms. Peck had placed a very
special bookmark there: one with a clown
holding up a ball with a number on it.

"Bingo!" I yelled. "Here it is!"

"Her bookmark smells just like rose perfume," said Teensie. She paused for a moment, then grinned. "Of course it does! That's because Ms. Peck was carrying it in her purse."

"Good smelling," I said.

"Good detective work," said Teensie. "Goofball, you're a genius."

Teensie was right. I was a genius. But there was no time to think about that now. We had to get that slip of paper to Pupu before the clock struck one.

We'd never hurried so fast. Everything we passed seemed happy. The paper flowers on the walls were smiling. The yellow sun hanging from the ceiling was beaming. Even the cafeteria smelled good.

Chapter 7: Ace Detective Spotted

We dashed into the classroom just as the bell rang.

"Did you find it?" everyone shouted.

"I hope so," said Pupu. He looked up at the clock just as the final bell rang. "Time just ran out."

I looked around the room. Everyone was waiting for my answer. I smiled. Everyone leaned forward.

"Well?" said Ms. Peck.

I waved the piece of paper over my head. "Check it out!"

Pupu quickly plucked the paper from my hand and studied the numbers. At last, he gave his blue nose a squeeze. *HONK!* "It's a winner!"

Ms. Peck nearly leaped onto her desk. Everyone clapped and yelled. Walter kicked up his leg and sent his shoe flying down the aisle. Pupu shook my hand and said, "How did you do it, Mr. Goofball?"

"The key to the mystery was that Ms. Peck was in a hurry in the library," I said. "The bell rang before she could write down the riddle. She must have been afraid she would forget it. So, she did what she always does when she needs to remember something. She used a bookmark."

Ms. Peck giggled. "I feel so silly," she said. "I used the only piece of paper I had in my purse. I didn't realize it was my winning number."

Teensie sniffed the air. "I can already smell the animals at the circus," she said. "Or is that Walter's sock?"

Walter quickly put his shoe back on.

Pupu bent down. He tapped Teensie's nose. "You've got a good sniffer there," he said.

Teensie gave Pupu's nose a squeeze. *HONK!* "Yours is pretty special, too."

Pupu smiled. Then he turned to me. "All right, Goofball, what was the answer to the riddle? Why can't the polka-dotted clown ever hide?"

"Simple," I replied. "A polka-dotted clown can't hide because he will always be spotted!"

Everyone laughed. Everyone but Ms. Peck. She giggled.

Pupu messed up my spiky hair. "You know what?" he said. "I've spotted something, too."

"You have?" I asked. "What?"

"An ace detective," he said. "And a very good riddler, too."

I grinned. Maybe I deserved to be the riddle king after all.